I Can Read!™ SHARED **My First** READING

THIS Biscuit
COLLECTION BELONGS TO:

_____

Dear Parent:
Your child's love of reading starts here!

Every child learns to read in a different way and at his or her own speed. Some go back and forth between reading levels and read favorite books again and again. Others read through each level in order. You can help your young reader improve and become more confident by encouraging his or her own interests and abilities. From books your child reads with you to the first books he or she reads alone, there are I Can Read Books for every stage of reading:

SHARED READING
Basic language, word repetition, and whimsical illustrations, ideal for sharing with your emergent reader

BEGINNING READING
Short sentences, familiar words, and simple concepts for children eager to read on their own

READING WITH HELP
Engaging stories, longer sentences, and language play for developing readers

READING ALONE
Complex plots, challenging vocabulary, and high-interest topics for the independent reader

ADVANCED READING
Short paragraphs, chapters, and exciting themes for the perfect bridge to chapter books

I Can Read Books have introduced children to the joy of reading since 1957. Featuring award-winning authors and illustrators and a fabulous cast of beloved characters, I Can Read Books set the standard for beginning readers.

A lifetime of discovery begins with the magical words **"I Can Read!"**

Visit www.icanread.com for information
on enriching your child's reading experience.

I Can Read Book® is a trademark of HarperCollins Publishers.

3 IN 1: I CAN READ! BISCUIT COLLECTION

This exclusive edition was printed for Kohl's Department Stores, Inc.
(for distribution on behalf of Kohl's Cares, LLC wholly owned) by HarperCollins Publishers.
For information address HarperCollins Children's Books, a division of
HarperCollins Publishers, 195 Broadway, New York, NY 10007.
www.icanread.com

ISBN: 978-0-06-285951-8

18 19 20 21 22 SCP 10 9 8 7 6 5 4 3 2 1

First Edition

Kohl's
Style number: 9780062859518
Factory Number 123386
05/2018

Biscuit

by ALYSSA SATIN CAPUCILLI
pictures by PAT SCHORIES

I Can Read!™

SHARED READING

My First READING

3

TREASURED STORYBOOKS

for Young Readers!

Biscuit Feeds the Pets

by ALYSSA SATIN CAPUCILLI • pictures by PAT SCHORIES

Bathtime for Biscuit

by ALYSSA SATIN CAPUCILLI • pictures by PAT SCHORIES

HARPER
An Imprint of HarperCollinsPublishers

TABLE OF CONTENTS

Biscuit
Page 9

Biscuit Feeds the Pets
Page 39

Bathtime for Biscuit
Page 69

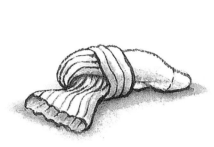

Biscuit

story by ALYSSA SATIN CAPUCILLI
pictures by PAT SCHORIES

For Laura and Peter who wait patiently
for a Biscuit of their very own
—A. S. C.

For Tess
—P. S.

This is Biscuit.
Biscuit is small.
Biscuit is yellow.

Time for bed, Biscuit!

Woof, woof!
Biscuit wants to play.

Time for bed, Biscuit!
Woof, woof!
Biscuit wants a snack.

Time for bed, Biscuit!
Woof, woof!
Biscuit wants a drink.

Time for bed, Biscuit!
Woof, woof!
Biscuit wants to hear a story.

Time for bed, Biscuit!
Woof, woof!
Biscuit wants his blanket.

Time for bed, Biscuit!
Woof, woof!
Biscuit wants his doll.

Time for bed, Biscuit!
Woof, woof!
Biscuit wants a hug.

Time for bed, Biscuit!
Woof, woof!
Biscuit wants a kiss.

Time for bed, Biscuit!
Woof, woof!
Biscuit wants a light on.

Woof!
Biscuit wants to be tucked in.

Woof!
Biscuit wants one more kiss.

Woof!
Biscuit wants one more hug.

Woof!

Biscuit wants to curl up.

Sleepy puppy.
Good night, Biscuit.

*For James, who loves to help
feed the pets!*
—A.S.C.

Biscuit Feeds the Pets

story by ALYSSA SATIN CAPUCILLI
pictures by PAT SCHORIES

Here, Biscuit.
We're going to help
Mrs. Gray today.
Woof, woof!

We're going to help
feed the pets!

Are you ready, Biscuit?
Woof, woof!

We can help feed
the fish, Biscuit.

We can help feed
the kittens, too.
Woof, woof!
Meow!

Wait, Biscuit!

Where are you going?

Woof, woof!
Yip—yip—yip!

Oh, Biscuit.
You found the new puppies!
Woof!

This way, Biscuit.
Woof, woof!

There are more pets
to feed over here.

Woof!
Biscuit!

Come out of there.

It's not time to play.

It's time to help Mrs. Gray.

Woof!
Yip!
Oh no, Biscuit!

Come back.
How will we feed
the pets now?

Woof, woof!

Yip—yip—yip!

Meow!

No, Biscuit, no.
Not the water bowl!

SPLASH!
Silly puppies!

Woof, woof!
Yip—yip—yip!

Funny puppy!

You found your own way to
help feed the pets, Biscuit.

You made lots of
new friends, too!

Meow!

Yip—yip—yip!

Woof, woof!

Bathtime for Biscuit

story by ALYSSA SATIN CAPUCILLI
pictures by PAT SCHORIES

This one is for my parents.
—A.S.C.

To Sri K.
—P.S.

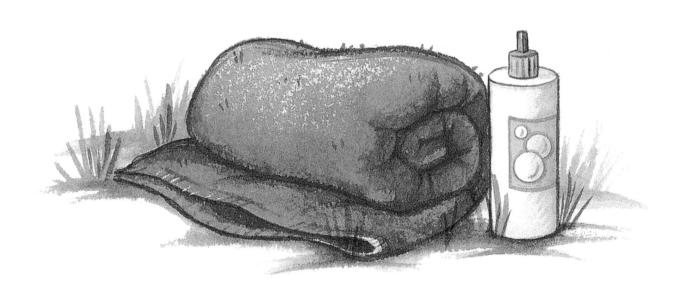

Time for a bath, Biscuit!
Woof, woof!
Biscuit wants to play.

Time for a bath, Biscuit!
Woof, woof!
Biscuit wants to dig.

Time for a bath, Biscuit!
Woof, woof!
Biscuit wants to roll.

Time for a bath, Biscuit!
Time to get nice and clean.
Woof, woof!

In you go!
Woof!
Biscuit does not want a bath!

Bow wow!
Biscuit sees
his friend Puddles.

Woof, woof!

Biscuit wants to climb out.

Come back, Biscuit!
Woof!

Come back, Puddles!
Bow wow!

Biscuit and Puddles
want to play
in the sprinkler.

Biscuit and Puddles
want to dig
in the mud.

Biscuit and Puddles
want to roll
in the flower bed.

Now I have you!

Woof, woof!
Let go of the towel,
Biscuit!

Bow wow!
Let go of the towel,
Puddles!

Silly puppies!

Let go!

Woof, woof!
Bow wow!

Oh!

Time for a bath, Biscuit!
Woof, woof!
A bath for all of us!